Five reasons why we you'll love this boo

Winnie AND Wilbur

THE BROOMSTICK RIDE

In the story Winnie and Wilbur try different ways to travel. Can you think of any other ways they should try?

There is so much to spot in every picture.

Wilbur meets a furry friend.

You can take the Winnie and Wilbur challenge: this book is full of planes but did you spot the train?

Contains a real pirate!

Freya

Anushka

Maggie

Bailey

Johannes

Molly

Ashley

Amber

Jun-Yeong

Pablo

Matilda

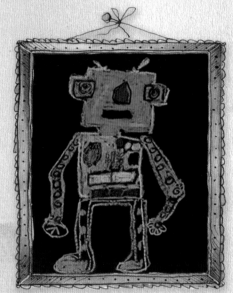

Marwin

Hasan

Rebecca

Thank you to all these schools for helping with the endpapers:

St Barnabas Primary School, Oxford; St Ebbe's Primary School,
Oxford; Marcham Primary School, Abingdon; St Michael's
C.E. Aided Primary School, Oxford; St Bede's RC Primary
School, Jarrow; The Western Academy, Beijing, China; John
King School, Pinxton; Neston Primary School, Neston; Star
of the Sea RC Primary School, Whitley Bay; José Jorge Letria
Primary School, Cascais, Portugal; Dunmore Primary School,
Abingdon; Özel Bahçeşehir İlköğretim Okulu, Istanbul, Turkey;
the International School of Amsterdam, the Netherlands;
Princethorpe Infant School, Birmingham.

For Sharon and Martin, who are
always full of good ideas—V.T.

For Ron Heapy—K.P.

OXFORD
UNIVERSITY PRESS

Great Clarendon Street, Oxford OX2 6DP

Oxford University Press is a department of the University of Oxford.
It furthers the University's objective of excellence in research, scholarship,
and education by publishing worldwide. Oxford is a registered trade mark of
Oxford University Press in the UK and in certain other countries

Text copyright © Valerie Thomas 1999
Illustrations copyright © Korky Paul 1999, 2016
The moral rights of the author and artist
have been asserted

Database right Oxford University Press (maker)

First published as *Winnie Flies Again* in 1999
This edition first published in 2016

British Library Cataloguing in Publication Data available

ISBN: 978-0-19-274821-8 (paperback)
ISBN: 978-0-19-274918-5 (paperback and CD)

10 9 8 7 6 5 4 3 2 1

Printed in China

Paper used in the production of this book is a natural, recyclable
product made from wood grown in sustainable forests. The
manufacturing process conforms to the environmental regulations
of the country of origin

www.winnieandwilbur.com

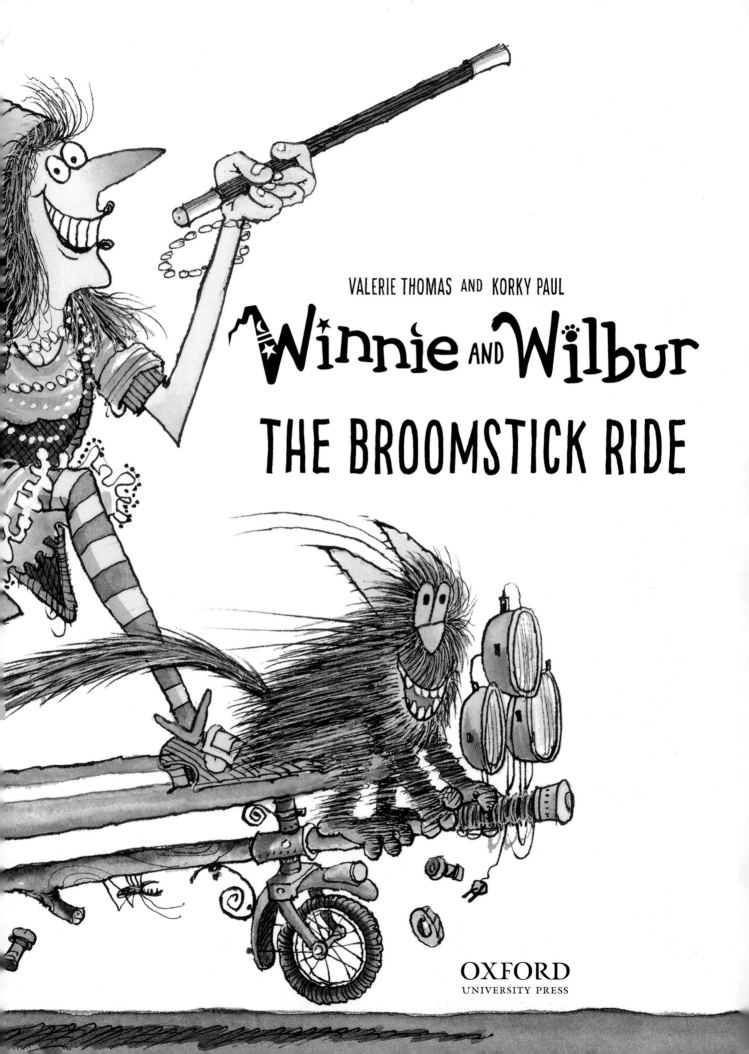

VALERIE THOMAS AND KORKY PAUL

Winnie AND Wilbur

THE BROOMSTICK RIDE

OXFORD
UNIVERSITY PRESS

Winnie the Witch always travelled by broomstick.
It was a wonderful way to travel.

Winnie would jump onto her broomstick.
Wilbur would jump onto her shoulder.
And they would zoom up into the sky.

There were no traffic lights.
No traffic jams.

Just the empty sky.

Well, that was how it used to be.
But, just lately, the sky had become
rather crowded.

Last week, Winnie didn't see a helicopter.
Wilbur lost two of his whiskers.

The week before that,
she didn't see a hang glider.

Wilbur's tail was bent.

The week before that, a very tall building suddenly got in her way.

Wilbur lost a clump of fur.

'The sky is too dangerous, Wilbur,' said Winnie.
'We'll have to try something else.'
So she took out her wand, waved it, and shouted,
'Abracadabra!'

Her broomstick turned into a
bicycle. But it was very slow.
Very hard to pedal.

And then a pond got in Winnie's way.
'She should look where she's going,' croaked a frog.

'A bicycle is worse than a broomstick, Wilbur,' said Winnie.
'We'll have to try something else.'
So she took out her wand, waved it, and shouted,

'Abracadabra!'

Her bicycle turned into a skateboard.
The skateboard was fast.
But it was hard to steer.
And impossible to stop.

Winnie was stopped. By an ice-cream seller.
'Can't you see where you're going?' he shouted.

'A skateboard is worse than a bicycle, Wilbur,' said Winnie.
'We'll have to try something else.'
So she took out her wand, waved it, and shouted,

'Abracadabra!'

Her skateboard turned into a horse,
and they trotted slowly down the path.
'This is much better than bicycles
or skateboards,' said Winnie.

But she didn't see . . .

. . . the low branch of a tree.
This time, Winnie didn't say anything.
She was hanging from a branch.

Slowly and carefully,
Winnie climbed down
from the tree.

'I think we'll walk
home, Wilbur,'
said Winnie.

They limped slowly along the road.
It was a very, very slow way to travel.

But it was safe.

Until Winnie stepped into a hole
and tumbled deep down under the ground.

YES
W ERE
E OPEN

'I think I need a
cup of tea,' Winnie said.

Winnie climbed out of the tunnel
and went into a shop.

'A cup of tea and a muffin, please,' she said.
'And a saucer of milk for my cat.'

'We don't sell cups of tea or muffins,'
said the shop lady.
'And we don't have saucers of milk.
But I think I can help you.'

And she sold Winnie a pair of spectacles.

Now, Winnie and Wilbur travel everywhere by broomstick.
It's a wonderful way to travel.

Bethany

Katia

Eun-Jae

Kathleen

Ji-Eun

Jenny

Sara

Fraser

Ka Keung

Selin

Selin

Olivia

Siyabend

Kieran

A note for grown-ups

Oxford Owl is a FREE and easy-to-use website packed with support and advice about everything to do with reading.

Informative videos

Hints, tips and fun activities

Top tips from top writers for reading with your child

Help with choosing picture books

For this expert advice and much, much more about how children learn to read and how to keep them reading ...

LOOK
for Oxford Owl
www.oxfordowl.co.uk